Money Doesn't Grow on Trees

by
Deletra Hudson, MBA

Illustrated by Donald L. Hill, MBA

Money Doesn't Grow on Trees

PUBLISHED BY:
Deletra Hudson, LLC
Copyright © 2016

Edited by Aja Dorsey Jackson

ISBN-13: 978-1530974658

Dedication

This book is dedicated to my three children, Jordan, Jada, and Anthony Jr., who are my inspiration for writing, living, loving and knowing the importance of creating and leaving legacies. They are my legacy keepers!

It was a beautiful spring day. All three of the kids were home from school. They were in their own rooms, doing their own thing, which gave me a minute to breathe and do nothing. I sat on the sofa to relax.

Suddenly, I heard someone running down the stairs. It was Joy, the oldest. She politely took a seat next to me on the sofa and interrupted my minute to breathe with her list of personal requests.

"Mom, while we are on spring break, I want to go to the movies to see a good scary movie," Joy began. "Now that I am 12 years old, I would like for you to let me go to the movies with my friend from school. Her name is Gabbie. After the movie, we plan to walk around inside of the mall for a little bit to kill time. Did I say that I want to do this without you being with us?"

"Excuse me Miss Joy, but I didn't hear you ask me if you could go to the movies and mall with Gabbie while you are on spring break!" I said. "I hear you demanding, very disrespectfully, about what you want to do. Furthermore, do you have any money to do these things?"

"Well, I was thinking you could buy our tickets for the movies. Oops...I mean, will you buy our tickets for the movies?" Joy replied. "By the way, I need another pair of school uniform pants so I can have a pair for each day of the week. I was planning on buying them when I went to the mall."

I looked at her like she said a bad word, then
I told her, "Girl, money doesn't grow on trees!"

"What makes you think I have extra money to take you and your friends to the movie theater, buy your tickets, and buy you pants for school while you are at the mall? I work hard every day to provide you, your little sister and little brother a place to live, clothes and shoes to wear, and even give you money for the extra things you want to do and have. It is time you understand how to appreciate and value money," I explained.

Joy tried to dismiss my statements. "But mom, I have my own money to buy popcorn and soda at the movies."

She had not understood a word of what I said.

"Joy, where did you get your money?" I asked.

"It's the money I got for birthday and Christmas presents," she responded.

"Ok. But that doesn't mean you have to spend it, just because you have it. How much money do you have from those presents?" I asked.

"I have seven dollars," Joy said proudly.

"Seven dollars!" I exclaimed, "You can't buy popcorn and soda at the movies with seven dollars." I laughed.

"Gabbie and I will split the cost of the popcorn and soda," she said with confidence. "That's why I was hoping you would help us out with buying the tickets to the movie. I'll do without the uniform pants for school if you let us go to the movies."

Since when did I get drawn into a negotiation with my 12-year-old daughter, who was very adamant about her plans? I thought. I felt there was no better time than the present to explain to her the importance of managing her money.

"Joy, learning how to manage your money is an important life skill. You cannot spend every penny you have," I started. "How much money will you have left to do other things if you spend all seven dollars at the movie theater?"

"I would have no money left," she responded.

"What will you have to show for spending all seven dollars on snacks at the movie theater?" I asked.

"My popcorn and soda," Joy said.

"But you and Gabbie plan to eat the popcorn and drink the soda. So, you will have nothing to show for your money when those things are gone," I explained. I finally had Joy's attention, so I continued my lesson. "When you only have a little money, you should not spend your last of it on things that do not add value to you."

I got up from the sofa and walked to the kitchen sink to get a glass of water. Joy followed. When I looked out of the window above the sink, I saw a vibrant green-leafed oak tree in the back yard.

I turned to Joy, who was now sitting at the kitchen table, and said, "I wish this old oak tree would grow dollar bills as its leaves. Then we would have money when we needed it while the tree was in bloom. But we don't live in a world where money grows on trees. Instead, we have to earn our money by working for it, just like you and your sister earn allowance for doing your chores around the house."

The moment those words left my mouth, in walked Joy's nine-year-old sister, Jay. "Mom, I am done sweeping and mopping the bathroom floor upstairs," Jay said. I reached into my pocket and handed Jay a $5 bill for completing the chores she was assigned for the week.

"Thanks, Mom! With these five dollars, I now have $185," she said proudly.

"Where did you get $185?" I asked Jay.

"I have been saving my money in my bank," she explained. "It is from the money I got for my birthday and Christmas presents, and the money you give me for doing my chores. Mom, I don't like to spend my money on stuff."

Then she looked at me with compassion in her eyes. "Do you need some money, MOM? I will loan you some, but you have to promise to pay it back," she said forcefully. "No thanks, Jay. I don't need any of your money," I replied with a smile. "You are doing a great job managing it. Keep up the good work.""Thanks, Mom!" Jay said, as she turned and ran off to her room.

As I walked back toward the kitchen table where Joy was still sitting, she whispered to me, "How did she save that much money?" I whispered back, "She doesn't spend her money as she gets it. She saves it by putting it away. When we go to the mall, she is fine with just walking around and spending time with her friends, you, and me. She doesn't always have to buy things." I looked into Joy's eyes and saw them light up. I could tell she was beginning to understand what I was saying.

"You see, Jay did her chores so she could continue to earn more money to add to her bank. She is not thinking about spending her money right now. I am not saying that you have to do what your little sister does, but you could learn to be more aware of what you do with your money as you get it," I further explained.

"You said you only had seven dollars and there is a sink full of dirty dishes to be cleaned. I see this as an opportunity for you to earn your allowance by doing the chores that have been assigned to you. Remember, you have to contribute to keeping the house clean."

Joy's eyes lit up like she struck gold. "You are right, Mom. I could wash the dishes, sweep and mop the kitchen floor and clean my room before the end of the week so I can have enough money to go the movies with Gabbie before our spring break is over," Joy said, full of excitement as she rushed to the kitchen sink to start washing the dishes.

I looked at Joy, feeling pleased that she understood. As I caught a glimpse of the oak tree through the kitchen window, Joy said, "Mom, don't worry about paying for our tickets. I will make enough money to buy my ticket, popcorn and soda. If there is any money left, I will save it for the next time I want to hang out with friends."

At that point, a feeling of relief came over me because I knew that in her own way, Joy understood my message very well. "That sounds like a plan my Big Girl." I smiled at Joy as I left the kitchen so that she could complete her chores.

Acknowledgements

I would like to first thank God for blessing me with the spirit of entrepreneurship and the courage to live my life out loud according to his will.

I have been blessed with an awesome family who always supports me in doing what I desire and helps me to follow my passions and live my life to the fullest.

Within those blessings, God gave me my husband Anthony, who supports my entrepreneurial journey and understands the importance of me following my calling to pursue my passion. He also helped me create my three beautiful children, Jordan, Jada and Anthony Jr., who inspire me to write and work hard to develop legacies for them, their future children, their children's children and other children in the world.

I am also grateful to the following people who continue to play their roles without expecting a Thank You. My expressions of gratitude outweigh any compensation I could ever give them:

My two sisters-cousins, Lori and Tanisha, who support me in all of my entrepreneurial ventures, including this book. Lori, who has served for more than 20 years as a schoolteacher in the Chicago Public School system, helped ensure that I was writing a children's book that was age-and-grade-level appropriate, and that the message was clear enough for children to understand and apply to their lives. Tanisha, my attorney cousin, was my pro bono proofreader. She made sure that the book was reflective of my intended message and the knowledge I wanted to convey to the reader.

My sister Tawnya is always my cheerleader. She understands how I feel when my entrepreneurial fire starts to burn because she also possesses that entrepreneurial spirit. I can count on her to help advertise and support the ventures of her "Little Big Sister."

My aunts, Donna and Barbara, who serve as the "mommy-fillers" to help raise my children to be people of substance and great contributors to this world.

My Heavenly Angels, my mom, dad and Granny, whom I know have been assigned to be a part of this entrepreneurial season of my life because I feel their presence paving the way and guiding me to experience my successful and abundant life, while whispering praises and expressing pride for my accomplishments.

Thank you to all of my family and friends who send me words of encouragement and congratulations on my life's journeys and accomplishments.

Lastly, I thank my business coach Brandy Butler, who encouraged me to pick up the draft of this book, which sat on a shelf for years, and to turn it into a published creation within three months.

Contact info:

deletra@deletrahudson.com
www.deletrahudson.com

Follow me:

Facebook Group- The Millionaire Inside Financial Empowerment Club
Twitter- @DeletraHudson
LinkedIn - Deletra Hudson
Instagram- deletra1